A NOTE ABOUT THE TRAIN

In the late thirties, when Beppy and Babs took the train to Lulu's, it was a two-railroad journey between Boston and Baltimore. A *New York, New Haven & Hartford R.R.* steam locomotive pulled the train from Boston to New Haven, where an electric locomotive took over and pulled the train into New York. At New York's Penn Station, the *Pennsylvania R.R.* took charge, and one of their electric locomotives pulled the train down to Baltimore. When the engine changed, so did the personnel, and a new conductor and engineer—among others— came aboard.

The change of engines was a smooth one, and many passengers were unaware of the switch because the same passenger cars were used by both companies. Beppy and Babs had the same comfortable seats for the whole trip.

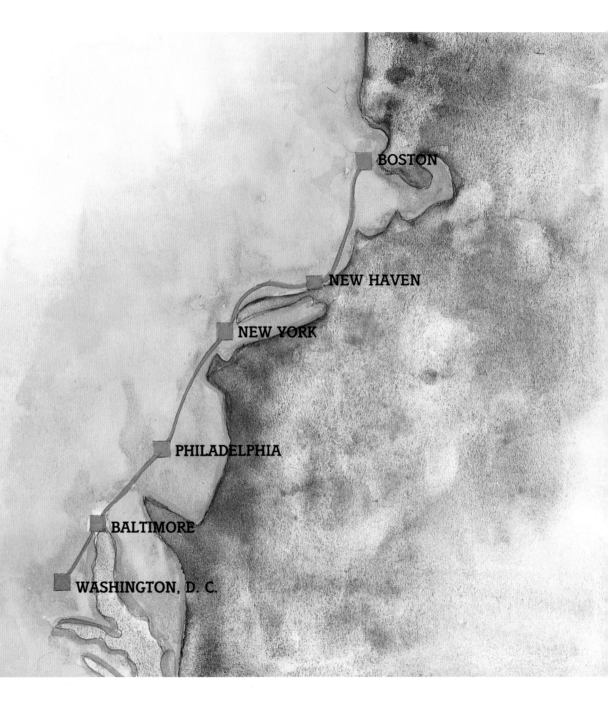

To my parents,
Mac and Bert Fitzgerald,
and to my sister, Barbara,
in happy memory of Lulu
and all those summers
--E.F.H.

To my son, Robert, Jr.
--R.C.

BOSTON

NEW HAVEN

NEW YORK

PHILADELPHIA

BALTIMORE

WASHINGTON, D. C.

THE TRAIN TO LULU'S

By Elizabeth Fitzgerald Howard

Illustrated by Robert Casilla

BRADBURY PRESS   NEW YORK

I'm happy! I'm happy! Today we are going on the train to Lulu's house! Babs and I! All by ourselves!

Mommy is packing our lunch and our supper for the train. I like it when Mommy says, "Beppy, you are a big girl now. You have to take care of Babs." It's a long, long ride from Boston to Baltimore. Nine hours!

Do we have everything? Our trunk and our suitcase, with clothes for the whole summer. Our paper dolls and crayons for the train.

Babs has her teddy bear. I have my book.

Oh, Daddy, don't forget our lunch boxes!

The Travelers' Aid lady says only Lulu will be able to take us away from the station in Baltimore, so Mommy and Daddy mustn't worry.

The conductors will watch out for us so we'll be sure to get off in Baltimore.

Babs looks like she might cry.
Daddy and Mommy are waving
good-bye. Now we are starting.

Oh, Babs! We are going to Lulu's house!
I can see a bridge! Do you see the water?
Boston is far, far now!

We are going so fast. Trees and houses are flying by.
I'm hungry. So is Babs. But Mommy said wait until the train
stops at New Haven. Then we can eat our lunch.

New Haven! New Haven! The
conductor is calling New Haven!

We open our lunch boxes. Surprise! A
Hershey bar for each of us. And chicken
sandwiches. Good lunch!

Here comes a man selling milk. We can buy some. Daddy gave us a dollar.

How much is the milk, please?

Ten cents.

We wobble around when we walk to the bathroom. The train is shaking. We have to hold on to the seats.

When will we get to Lulu's house?

Every minute Babs asks me that. She is too little to understand that trains take a long time.

We play with our paper dolls. We draw pictures.

I draw a train. Babs draws a funny teddy bear.

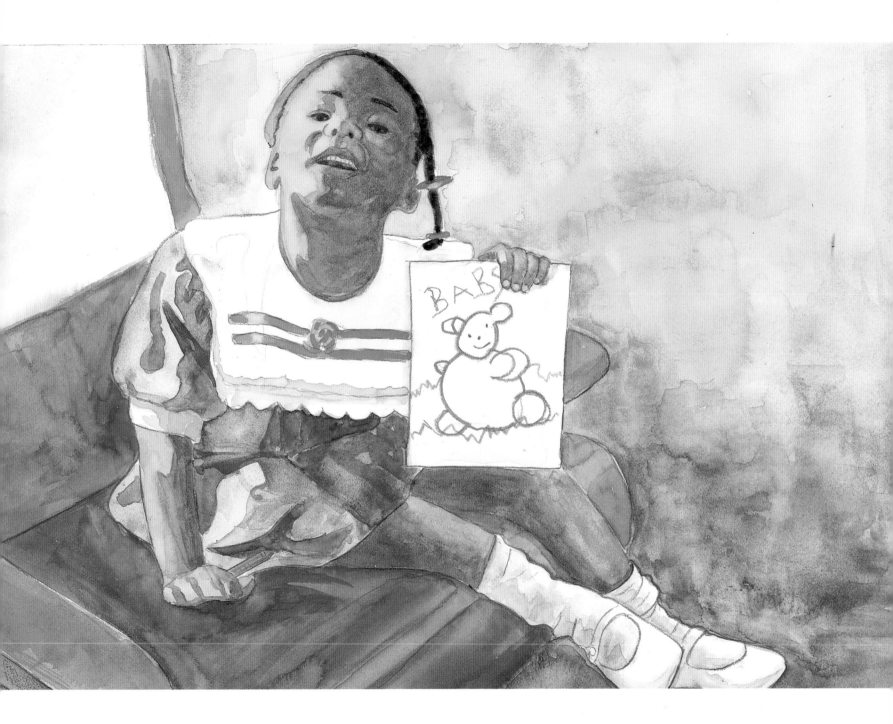

We look out our window. Now we are in New York!
Babs is hungry again. Mommy said wait until Philadelphia
to eat our supper sandwiches.
But when is Philadelphia?

Look, Babs. There's a new conductor.
Philadelphia! Philadelphia! He's
calling Philadelphia!

Oh, we have molasses sandwiches
and a carrot and a cookie for each of
us. Good supper!

I want to read my book.

When will we get to Lulu's house?

Babs must be tired. She is acting like a silly baby and bouncing up and down.

Babs, stop that! I will tell you a story so you can be good. I will tell you *The Babes in the Wood.*

. . .

When the children got lost in
the woods they fell asleep on
the ground. And the robins
covered them all up with
leaves.

Oh, no, Babs! Don't wake up! We
won't get lost! We are going to
Lulu's house!

Babs, you mustn't cry. People are looking at us.
You really are a baby.
All right, here's your teddy bear. We have to be good.
Now Babs is asleep again.
It's getting a little dark out. I don't want to read anymore.
When will we get to Lulu's house?

Baltimore! Baltimore! Next stop Baltimore!

The conductor is telling us we must be ready to get off.

Babs, wake up!

I take our suitcase and my book. Babs takes her
teddy bear.

The conductor slides our trunk down for us.

We step off the train.

Babs, look! Aunt Flossie and Uncle
Howard! And Aunt Eva! And Aunt Erma
and Uncle Brad! And Chita!

Another Travelers' Aid lady is here.
She says everybody has to wait
for Lulu.

All the aunts and uncles hug and kiss us. So many hugs and kisses!
They say we are very smart girls. But where is Lulu?

I see someone coming with white, white hair! Lulu is here!

Lulu, Lulu! We came on the train! We are going to your house for the whole summer!